P9-AZV-858

orca
limelights

HE WHO DREAMS

Melanie Florence

ORCA BOOK PUBLISHERS

Library and Archives Canada Cataloguing in Publication

Florence, Melanie, author
He who dreams / Melanie Florence.
(Orca limelights)

Issued in print and electronic formats.
ISBN 978-1-4598-1102-7 (paperback).—ISBN 978-1-4598-1103-4 (pdf).—
ISBN 978-1-4598-1104-1 (epub)

I. Title. II, Series: Orca limelights
PS8611.L668H42 2017   jC813'.6   C2016-904459-9
                                              C2016-904460-2

First published in the United States, 2017
Library of Congress Control Number: 2016949037

Summary: In this high-interest novel for teen readers, a soccer star surprises
everyone by signing up for Indigenous dance classes.

*Orca Book Publishers is dedicated to preserving the environment and has printed
this book on Forest Stewardship Council® certified paper.*

Orca Book Publishers gratefully acknowledges the support for
its publishing programs provided by the following agencies:
the Government of Canada through the Canada Book Fund and the Canada
Council for the Arts, and the Province of British Columbia through the BC
Arts Council and the Book Publishing Tax Credit.

Cover design by Rachel Page
Cover photography by iStock.com

ORCA BOOK PUBLISHERS
www.orcabook.com

Printed and bound in Canada.

20 19 18 17 • 4 3 2 1

For my family—Chris, Josh and Taylor.

One

The math book flew across the room and hit the wall before landing facedown on the floor. I rubbed my eyes and shook my head in frustration. I loathed math. I could never remember formulas or equations. And, to be honest, I had never actually bothered to memorize the multiplication tables.

My mom poked her head in the door.

"What was that?" she asked.

I gestured wordlessly at the textbook.

She smiled. "Ah. Math again?"

I nodded. "I just don't get it! My brain doesn't work that way." I pushed the hair off my forehead and sighed deeply.

"Mine never did either, *nikosis*," my mom told me, walking across the room to pick up my math book and putting it back on my desk. "Which is why our resident engineer, also known as your father, does our taxes. Maybe he can go over your homework with you in the morning." She stood behind me and ruffled my hair. She always loved playing with my hair, so different from her own jet-black mane. Auburn, she called it. Like a *pahkisimon*. A sunset. Really, it was just red.

"Yeah, maybe." I shrugged. I had to maintain decent grades to stay on the soccer team, so, much as I hated to admit it, I couldn't let my math homework slide.

"All right, I'm off to bed." My mom kissed me on the cheek and headed out the door. She stopped suddenly. "Oh, I almost forgot!"

"What?" I asked, stretching and standing up to get ready for bed.

"I have a meeting with clients tomorrow afternoon. You don't have soccer tomorrow, do you?"

"Nope," I answered. "What do you need? And if you want me to go grocery shopping again, I reserve the right to add whatever I want to the shopping list."

"Not a chance!" My mom threw her head back and laughed loudly. "You cost me $50 the last time you went shopping, nikosis."

I smiled wryly. "Sorry about that. So what did you want me to do?"

"Can you take your sister to her art class after school tomorrow?" she asked.

"Yeah, I guess." I shrugged. "At the community center?"

"Yes. Thanks, sweetie. I really appreciate it. Get some sleep, okay?" She blew a kiss and grabbed my laundry hamper before heading out of my room, closing the door behind her.

I sighed and pulled my T-shirt off, tossing it absentmindedly into the corner where my hamper usually sat. My dad better be able to work his magic before my math test on Thursday, or I'd be benched.

Two

The next morning at the kitchen table I was right back where I'd started, staring blankly at my math book, when my dad walked in and poured himself a cup of coffee.

"Need some help?" he asked, falling heavily into the chair beside me.

"Yeah." I tilted the page toward him so he could see what I was working on.

He ran a hand through his hair—red like mine—and frowned down at it. "Here." He tapped the paper in front of me. "This is where you went wrong." He circled what looked like a random bunch of numbers. "You used the wrong formula," he said.

For the next forty minutes, my dad patiently explained the finer points of quadratic equations.

He made it look easy. It wasn't. But I kind of understood it by the time we were done.

"Thanks, Dad. I think I've got it. I don't know how you keep all those equations straight."

"I'm Irish! It's in my blood." He winked at me.

"Yeah, well...I'm half Irish, and it doesn't appear to be in mine."

"Sometimes I suspect you've got more of your mother's Cree blood in you than my Irish." He laughed.

"Not to look at us," I said. I looked exactly like my dad and absolutely nothing like my mom. It was a little awkward sometimes. The people on the rez where my mom grew up had known me all my life, but it wasn't always that easy. Back in fifth or sixth grade, we were learning about Aboriginal history, and the teacher asked if any of us knew any Aboriginal people. I raised my hand to tell the class that my mom was Aboriginal. The teacher, not having met my mother, told me to stop lying. In front of the entire class. When I told my mother about it later, she was furious and threatened to come to school with me the next day to confront him. I was mortified, but she had a point. The fact that I looked like my Irish father and not her didn't make me any less Indigenous than my sister, who was a carbon copy of my mom.

"You may look like me, John, but you're so much like your mom," my dad said.

I wasn't sure whether this was true—but my mom was artistic and fiery and sweet and proud, and I was happy to be compared to her. Even if people couldn't often tell that she was my mother.

Three

"It's in here!" Jen pulled on my arm, practically dragging me down the hall and into a bright room filled with easels, pottery wheels and desks covered in pencils and markers. "The class is an hour, so come back and get me at five, okay?" She darted into the room and grabbed a smock from a hook on the wall before I could answer.

"Okay. So, five o'clock. Right here," I called to no one in particular. Jen was already out of earshot. Or just ignoring me. It was hard to tell which. I turned to leave.

"Five thirty!" Jen yelled at my back.

"Fine." I waved a hand in the air as I left. Great. An hour and a half. No homework. No book. How was I supposed to kill ninety minutes?

I pulled my phone out of my back pocket and scrolled through my apps. None appealed to me. Not Mega Jump. Not Mad Coaster. Not even Temple Run. Or Cut the Rope. Nothing. And my battery was down to 15 percent, so I couldn't listen to music. Sighing, I put my phone away and looked around. The Community Center halls were quiet. All of the classes had already started. I leaned back against the wall. My watch now read *4:05*. Great. Five minutes down and only eighty-five to go. I clicked my tongue. I rolled my eyes. I snapped my fingers and drummed on the wall. Finally I stuck my hands in my pockets and started wandering aimlessly down the hall.

I bounced around a little, poking my head into the door of a prenatal yoga class and stood in the back of an Alcoholics Anonymous meeting before realizing what was happening and slinking out, my mouth full of the chocolate-chip cookies that had been on the table in the back. I wiped my mouth with the back of my hand, swallowed the last bite... and heard the sound of drums and what sounded like chanting coming from somewhere to my left.

I followed the drumbeat down the hall to an unmarked door. I looked around and, seeing no one, pulled it open and slipped inside. The drum was much louder here. It was punctuated by the sound of feet stomping and a woman's voice calling out instructions. I edged forward, finding myself at the back of a stage overlooking a gymnasium.

"Lighter feet, Julie. That's great. Okay, ladies, twirl and twirl and twirl!" Chanting voices shrieked in time with the drumbeat, and I walked forward until I reached the edge of the stage and ducked behind the curtain. Taking a deep breath, I peered around the curtain at a group of girls dancing. I had been to Pow Wows back on the rez with my mom, but I had never paid much attention to the people there shuffling along to the music. I'd grown up around them, and although I had always liked the music well enough, I had spent my time at the Pow Wows with the other boys, eating fry bread and flirting with the girls. But this was different somehow. The energy was different.

Like the people on the rez, these girls were dressed in every color imaginable. Each had her hair braided and wore a headband sprouting feathers and beads. All were wearing moccasins and elaborate shawls with long fringes that matched their intricately beaded dresses. The girls held their shawls out, twirling and whirling madly, like mini dervishes. Their feet were a blur of motion as they stomped softly across the floor, tapping and weaving their way around the room. I watched, unaware that I was holding my breath.

"Girls, feel the music. Feel the drums. This is the dance of your ancestors! Taylor, drop your shoulder a little more on the turn," the woman called out, turning and catching sight of me watching sneakily from behind the curtain. Our eyes met and I jumped back, heart pounding. I stood away from the curtain, waiting for the woman to call me out. "All right ladies, keep twirling!" I backed toward the door, inching my way out, and made my way down the hall toward Jen's art class.

"Hey!" a voice called out behind me.

Damn! Almost made it. I turned, hands up.

"Look, I'm sorry," I blurted out. "I didn't mean to interrupt your class." I was backing up as she advanced. "It won't happen again."

She laughed kindly at me. "Stop. It's fine. Look, I saw you watching the class. I know you, don't I?" she asked.

"No, I don't think so." I turned to leave.

"The rez is a small place. You're William Greyeyes grandson, right?"

I stared at her, surprised. "Uh...yeah. How did...have we met?" I stammered.

"No. But I've seen you around. William's redheaded grandson." She laughed at that. "Do you dance?"

Now it was my turn to laugh. "Me? No. Not at all."

"Really? You seemed to be enjoying the music. I just wanted to invite you to try the class."

"What? Why?" I looked at her in shock. "Thanks, really. But I don't dance. I'm an athlete, not a dancer. I play soccer. And hockey. And lacrosse. But I don't dance. Sorry." I smiled. I was about to walk away when the teacher started laughing.

"An athlete, huh?" she asked, smirking. "Okay." She started digging in her bag, pulled out a DVD and held it out to me. "Just watch this. If you're not interested, fine. But if you want to try it, come back, and you can give it a shot." She waved the DVD in front of me.

I reached out and took it from her, not wanting to be rude. "I'm Santee," she said, smiling.

"John McCaffrey. Thanks."

She nodded and turned back toward the gym. I watched her walk away and then glanced down at my watch. "Oh no..." I started to run toward Jen's art class, clutching the DVD tightly in my hand.

Four

Dinner dragged on forever. I had only taken Santee's DVD to be polite, but I had to admit, I was curious to get upstairs with my laptop to watch it. I was dying to see why she had laughed when I said I was an athlete. Finally the meatloaf and mashed potatoes were consumed, and I was pushing back my chair to escape to my room. I grabbed a handful of Oreos on the way through the kitchen.

"John, can you clear the table for me, please?" my mother called out. *Ugh. So close!* I did a quick U-turn and grabbed the plate out from under Jen.

"Hey!" she protested.

"You're done." I grinned and stuck my tongue out at her and stacked all the plates together, throwing her a cookie. She caught it deftly and held her fork out to me. "Thanks a lot, Your Highness," I said and bowed.

She smirked back at me, chocolate-cookie crumbs in her teeth.

"Nice, Jen." I laughed, then carried the dirty dishes into the kitchen and loaded the dishwasher.

"Thanks, nikosis." My mom kissed my cheek and ruffled my hair.

"No problem. Do you need me to do anything else? Wash the floor? Do the laundry?" I joked, straight-faced.

"Well, now that you mention it..."

I smiled as I walked out of the kitchen. I closed my bedroom door behind me, grabbed my head-phones and pushed the DVD into my laptop. Within seconds, the drumbeats began. I watched as the credits rolled down the screen. *Exhibition of Nations Pow Wow 2016 Men's Traditional Fancy Dance Competition.* Wait...men's dance? I leaned in as the drums sped up and the warbling voices rose. The screen went dark suddenly, and I found myself holding my breath, waiting. Moments later a splash of color lit up the screen. The music swelled, and an elaborately costumed man leaped into view.

This was nothing like the Pow Wows back on the rez. I had never seen anything like this in my life. I sat back hard, my eyes glued to the screen as the man jumped, seemed to hover and then twirled at lightning speed. He dropped to one knee and spun, pushed himself around with the other foot, and leaped back to his feet. I had never thought of dancers as athletic, but Santee was right. There was no other word for it. Proud and strong, the man danced fiercely, never pausing. He was a constant blur of powerful motion. With his face painted and his feathered costume flying around him, he looked like a warrior. I couldn't take my eyes off him.

As the music and the dance came to a stop, I let out a long breath. There was something about that music that...well, it called to me, stupid as that might sound. I *felt* it. I wanted to be that fierce-looking man. For the first time in my life, it occurred to me that a man dancing didn't have to look like my Uncle Deke, who had absolutely no rhythm and who inevitably ended up falling over at some point during any given song.

I slowly closed my laptop and laid my headphones on top of it. I leaned back in my chair and stared out my bedroom window. The sun sank lower and lower in the sky. Hands linked behind my head, I tried to picture myself leaping and twirling in costume.

It was easier to picture than I had imagined.

Five

The next day passed in a blur of classes, friends and daydreams. I was a bundle of nerves. On one hand, I was eager to talk to Santee about the DVD she had loaned me. But on the other hand, I wasn't quite sure what to say without sounding like a complete idiot. I had visions of myself shuffling my feet, muttering under my breath with my eyes on the floor. *Umm, yeah...so that dancing guy? He's cool.* I felt like crawling under my desk just thinking about it.

The closer it got to the end of the day, the more nervous I became. My neck was hot and itchy, and I had my hand snaked down the back of my collar, scratching. I always got itchy when

I was stressed out. The bell rang, surprising me, and I let out a little shriek, jumping out of my desk. Thankfully, it was so loud with everyone filing out of the room that no one heard me. I rose shakily to my feet, grabbed my bag and headed to the lower school to pick up my sister. Her school was attached to mine by a covered walkway, which came in real handy in the winter.

Jen was waiting when I got to her class. "Let's go!" She grabbed my hand, pulling me toward the door. "If I finish my projects, I can take them home today."

"Okay, okay. I'm coming." I laughed. She was like a little tornado. Always moving. Always excited about her latest project. Always smiling. She'd be a great dancer, I thought, glancing at her as we got into the car and headed to the community center. She fiddled with the radio as I drove, singing a line here and there and then immediately changing the station again.

"Jen, pick a station, would you?" I begged.

She sighed deeply. "I was looking for Taylor Swift. Or at the very least, One Direction. Or maybe One Republic. Mom has the radio set to easy listening. *Easy listening*, John!"

We pulled into the parking lot of the center. "Sorry, Jen. We'll bring CDs next time. Hey!" I yelled as she jumped out of the car.

"It's okay. I'm going in. Pick me up at five." She yanked the door to the center open. "No! Five thirty! I want to finish my projects!"

"Look both ways next time," I shouted out the window. She rolled her eyes and disappeared inside before I was even out of the car. I shook my head. Yep. She was a whirlwind, all right. I grabbed the DVD and lurched out of the car, slamming the door behind me. I took a deep breath and headed after my sister and into the center.

Rounding the corner to the gym, I was greeted by the now-familiar music and the dance teacher calling out to her students.

"No, Lily. You need to go to the left, not the right. Good! Much better." The door was propped open, so I braced myself and stood in the doorway. Santee caught my eye after a minute and started toward me. "Keep going, ladies, that's great! You're one beat behind, Eden. That's better." She stopped in front of me and raised her eyebrows. "So? What did you think?"

I tried to be cool. For about five seconds.

"It was amazing!" I blurted out, smiling widely. "I've never seen anything like it. I want to do that! I want to be that guy!"

Santee laughed at my enthusiasm and patted me on the back. "Okay then." She studied my face for a moment. "So...want to come in and give it a try?"

Six

"**O**kay, ladies, facing forward. This is John, and he's going to watch what you do and follow along. It's his first class, and he's just another student today, so let's go easy on him, okay? So everyone say hi and then forget he's here."

"Hi, John!" The girls giggled and stared at me.

Santee turned to me. "So traditionally, you'd learn to dance by following the older dancers and doing what they do. But since you're the oldest person here, you'll follow the more experienced dancers." She waved a hand around the room while the girls laughed and poked each other.

"Hi." I waved, my cheeks burning. They were all staring, so I tried to think of what made my sister laugh and did a low, theatrical bow to the class. They collapsed against each other in fits of giggles.

"Okay then," Santee said. "Facing forward. You too, Taylor. So, John, just try to follow along. We'll keep it simple and take it slow."

I nodded, shifting my weight nervously from foot to foot.

"Great. Okay...music! And let's start with a simple step and step and—knees higher, John. Good! Feel the music, class. I want to see everyone floating." Santee stepped in front of me. "It's a little different for men. Instead of that single step they're doing, you want to do kind of a double step. Don't put your heel down, but land on the ball of your foot. So lower your heel, but don't let it touch. No, don't let it touch. You're letting it touch."

"Okay, okay." I looked up at her, then back down.

"Stop looking at your feet! Chin up. Shoulders back. You should be dancing with your whole body even when you're just doing simple steps. And stay light on your feet. This is how we'd dance in a Grand Entry at Pow Wow." She looked at me, probably trying to gauge how much I knew about Pow Wows, before continuing. "John, at a

Pow Wow the area we dance in is called the arbor. It's sacred. The arbor is a special place where all of your good thoughts come back to you. If you dance unselfishly—for someone other than yourself, for someone who can't dance or who is suffering—if you can do that, you will truly feel the music and dance better than you've ever danced before."

I nodded and tried to remember not to put my heels down. She turned away as the music sped up. I fixed my eyes on the girls dancing in a line ahead of me and did my best to mimic what they were doing.

I watched intently, but their feet were moving so fast! And, as it turned out, I had absolutely no coordination at all. I tried stepping as lightly as the girls, but the fact that my steps were echoing off the walls was a little off-putting. And I kept forgetting to add the second tap of my foot that the girls didn't have. I thought I was starting to get the hang of it when Santee changed it up on me.

"And let's spin! Same steps, John, but we're going to add a simple spin...now!"

I looked up, panicking, and spun to the left as everyone else twirled right. I tried to correct myself at the last second, and my feet somehow got tangled together, sending me crashing to the gymnasium floor. I heard the girls laughing around me, but I couldn't bring myself to look. A small hand reached down in front of my burning face. I glanced up at the tiny girl standing over me, her glossy hair in braids and a crooked grin on her face. She smiled bigger, still holding out her hand. As humiliated as I was, I couldn't help but laugh. She reminded me of my sister.

As I reached out and took her hand, she leaned down and whispered in my ear. "Don't worry. I fell down in my first class too."

"Really?" I asked, smiling.

"Yep." She stood with me as I rose to my feet. "Just watch me," she said. "I'll show you what to do."

The rest of the class had continued without us, so I brushed myself off and nodded at her. "Okay. Ready. Wait! What's your name?"

"Taylor. Okay. So bounce...just bounce."

I bounced on the balls of my feet. This was easy! Once I got the hang of that, I nodded at my mini teacher to continue.

"Good! Now step...you want to almost skip. But it's not a skip." She giggled at her description. "So bounce and bring your foot up and then step." I followed her. "That's great! Now try it in time to the drums."

I had completely forgotten to listen to the drums. I had forgotten everything except watching my little friend as she slowly started to turn.

"Whoa...okay. Hang on a sec." I took a deep breath and followed. I did it!

"Good job!" I heard Santee call out. I beamed and kept dancing.

"Go, John!" Taylor clapped. I spun harder. The whole class was clapping now. I was feeling pretty cocky at this point and kept spinning. Kept stepping. Kept lifting my knees. Kept listening to the drumbeats.

"Stop!" I vaguely heard someone call out, but it barely registered. I was on a roll. I was dancing! I was doing great...until I hit a cart full of basketballs and went down hard, hitting my shin and my hip on the way down.

The class ran over, hovering and cooing over me like miniature mother hens.

"Are you okay?" Taylor asked.

I rubbed my leg, grinning despite the pain. "I'm good. Did you see that? I was doing it!" I couldn't stop smiling.

Santee grabbed my hand and hauled me up. "Well done, John. It's a good start."

Taylor reached over and high-fived me. "Just wait until next week," she told me. "We'll try adding a jump."

* * *

After an hour of me stumbling my way through a series of steps and trying my best to keep up with the whirling dervishes that were the little girls spinning around me, I felt like my head was spinning around with them. They giggled their way out the door at the end of the class as I gathered up my things and tried to ignore the growing aches and pains in my body.

"You did well today, John." Santee was collecting her own things and getting ready to leave. "Did you enjoy it?"

"I did," I admitted, stretching my back and feeling a twinge of pain. It was going to hurt a lot later.

"I'm glad," Santee said, heading for the door.

"It's just..." I called out to her back, then watched her turn and look at me quizzically.

"It's just what?" she asked.

"Well, I think I'd like to come back, but I was wondering if there was a class for boys."

"Ah." Santee nodded. "I guess it must feel a bit awkward being in a class of little girls."

"Kind of, yeah."

"But unless you can drive into the city, mine is the only class around here," she explained. "I'm sorry."

"Okay. That's all right. I just wondered," I said.

She turned back toward the door. "See you next week," I called after her.

I couldn't see how I could get to the city to take a dance class. I supposed I could ask to borrow the car. But then I'd have to explain why, and I felt like I had to see if this was something I really wanted to do before I told my parents. I had run through a long list of hobbies and sports, only to grow bored as soon as my parents had shelled out for equipment and supplies. Art classes, drama, football,

hockey, a short-lived interest in scuba diving...
it was a long list. Other than soccer, nothing
had stuck for me.

No. I was going to pay for these lessons out
of my own money and see where the adventure
took me before I told my family.

Seven

"Owww!" I limped into the locker room and immediately hit my already aching hip against a huge rolling bin full of towels. "Ouch! Damn it!" I hopped around on one foot, rubbing my leg furiously. I tripped over a gym bag and just barely missed landing in Raymond's lap.

"Hey!" Raymond playfully shoved me away. "Get off me."

I landed on the bench and rolled my eyes as the team laughed.

"Right where you belong, McCaffrey...riding the bench." Tyler, our fearless goalie, threw a towel at my head.

I caught it deftly and threw it back. Tyler missed it and turned red as the team cracked up.

"Maybe John should be playing goal, Ty!" Raymond called out.

"Ha-ha. Very funny," Tyler called back, throwing his cleat toward Raymond's head. It went wide, and I reached out and caught that too. The team whooped with laughter and shouted catcalls at Tyler.

"Oh, shut up," he told them as I took an elaborate bow, wincing at the pain radiating from basically everywhere on my body.

"Ouch," I muttered. I opened my locker, pulled off my sweats and reached for my uniform.

"What the hell happened to you?" Aiden asked, glancing at the huge bruise on my leg.

"What...oh, that?" I shrugged and tried to think of a plausible explanation. I could only imagine the reaction my teammates would have to my dancing. "Pickup basketball game last night. Things got a little rough. I took an elbow to the stomach and went down hard."

"Yeah. Apparently," Aiden said, eyebrows raised. "You okay to play?"

"Just try to stop me," I said, pulling on my uniform and sitting down to lace up my cleats, trying to pretend that my leg wasn't throbbing.

Tanner stalked into the room, fully dressed, a scowl darkening his features. "We're up against one of the best teams in the city today. We need to be better than them, right?" he yelled.

"Yeah!" we shouted back.

"We need to be faster than them, right?"

"Yeah!" we all yelled.

"We need to be smarter than them, right?"

"Yeah!"

"Then let's get out there and win this game!" Tanner shouted.

"YEAH!" We jumped up and followed him out of the locker room and onto the soccer field.

Central Tech was tough. They were widely recognized as one of the best, if not *the* best team in the city—and they weren't above playing dirty if it would help them win the game. We had played them before, and I had spent the better part of one of those games on the bench because one of their players had taken me out with an elbow to the face. I was sore today, but I was ready to play. Or I thought I was. I suddenly yawned so big, it felt like my face was about to split in half.

"Dude!" Aiden elbowed me in the ribs. "Don't let Tanner see you yawning like that."

"Yeah, sorry. Just nerves or something, I guess," I told him, mentally slapping myself awake. Luckily, Tanner had been chatting with the coach, and neither one of them saw the yawn. I got down on the ground with Aiden and started stretching to warm up my muscles for the game. It hurt. A lot. But as I looked over at the other team and saw the little weasel who had taken me out of the last game cackling with his buddies, I knew that I was going to work through the pain if it killed me. I shot a dirty look across the field and tried to work out the kinks. I had a feeling that all the stretching in the world wasn't going to make much of a difference today.

The game started, and I did my best to keep up with the rest of the team, but judging by the constant barrage of trash talk Tanner kept throwing my way, I wasn't doing a very good job of it. I saw the guy from the other team heading right at me with the ball and a cocky look on his face. There was no way I could let him get past me. I veered off, and within seconds I was facing him. I put my head down and rushed toward him, fully intending to either steal the ball or take him down. The other player faked left, and I shadowed him, moving closer. No way was this guy getting past me!

"Stay on him, McCaffrey!" Tanner shouted. "Get the ball!"

I looked toward Tanner, and in that instant the weasel weaved around and shot right past me.

"Damn it!" Tanner screamed. "Get him!"

My face burned. It was Tanner's fault for distracting me! I would have had him if Tanner had just kept his mouth shut for ten seconds! I changed direction and took off after the other player, who was getting dangerously close to the goal. My legs ached as I dug deep and tore across the field.

"Go, John!" I heard Aiden call out from somewhere off to the right. I didn't look up. I didn't even turn my head a little. I focused on the other player and kept running. I caught him about twenty meters away from the goal. The weasel saw me coming and paused slightly, gauging the distance to the net. I dove toward him, going for the ball just as he did a fancy side step and completely avoided me. I slid right past the ball as it flew toward the net.

"Noooooo!" Tanner screamed. I had a faceful of grass and what felt like a rug burn on my knee as I turned with the rest of the team to watch the ball soaring directly toward Tyler. Effortlessly, the goalie jumped and grabbed the ball out of the air.

"Yes!" I yelled, throwing a fist into the air in victory. Tyler had just won us the game. I hated that I had eaten dirt trying to get the ball from the idiot on the other team, but at least Tyler was on top of it. Literally.

The team ran past and crowded around Tyler. Aiden stopped beside me and offered a hand up.

"Good try." He smiled.

"Thanks." I took his hand and winced at the new bruise forming on my other leg.

The coach bounded over. "Way to go, boys! Good game."

"Yeah, no thanks to McCaffrey," Tanner muttered as he stalked past Aiden and me.

I opened my mouth to tell him he shouldn't have distracted me, but the truth was, if I'd been playing well, nothing Tanner said would have kept me from getting that ball.

"Come on. I could use a shower," I told Aiden, limping slightly as we headed for the locker room.

Eight

"**O**kay, girls, arms out! A little softer on your feet, Carli. That's right. Perfect!" Santee weaved through the dancing girls, making her way toward me. I was trying desperately to keep up and copy what Taylor was doing effortlessly beside me. I grunted with pain as I lost my balance, thanks to my still-sore legs. I stumbled and was shoved back into position by Taylor, who grinned good-naturedly.

"Rough night?" she asked.

"Wise guy," I gasped. "I was all sore from trying to dance and then I had soccer practice. Coach has been running us ragged to get us ready for the game tomorrow."

"Excuses, excuses," she called over her shoulder as she twirled away, sticking her tongue out at me playfully. That kid was a force of nature, I thought, sticking my tongue out back at her. She giggled.

"Very nice, Taylor." Santee beamed at her. "Don't forget—the shawl should look like a butterfly's wings. Hold it softly, like this." Santee demonstrated for the girls. "Now step lightly. Feel the music. Flutter, girls. Flutter!"

I stifled a laugh as the girls fluttered behind their teacher, colorful shawls held aloft as they danced in a long rainbow line. Then a lone dancer entered my peripheral vision. It was Taylor, and she wasn't fluttering. She wasn't following the line of girls across the room. But like the other dancers, she held her pink-and-blue shawl high above her head while she spun. Taylor turned suddenly and leaped through the air, her back arched, a look of utter joy on her face. She landed as the last beat of the drum sounded and stopped, her chest heaving as the entire class stared. I burst into applause, followed by the rest of the dancers.

Santee bounded over and hugged her, then held her at arm's length. "Where did that come from?" she asked, smiling broadly at Taylor.

Taylor shrugged as she gulped for air. "I heard it in the music," she managed to say.

I didn't hear Santee's response. I was too busy gaping at the clock. Soccer practice had started fifteen minutes ago. I groaned. If I left right now, I'd be half an hour late. Coach was going to kill me. Then the team would take turns kicking my butt on the field. I headed to where I had dumped my backpack and threw it over my shoulder. The music started up behind me, and Santee called for the girls to start fluttering around the room again. I turned to the door just as she reached my side.

"Going somewhere?" she asked.

"Yeah. Soccer practice. I'm already late," I told her, gesturing toward the clock.

She nodded. "Listen, John. I wanted to talk to you about something..."

"Okay. But can it wait?" I asked, glancing at the clock and shifting my bag to my other shoulder. "I'm sorry, Santee, but I really have to go."

"All right, but just one thing." She handed me a flyer with a photo of a fierce-looking man on it.

"What's this?" I asked.

"It's the Pow Wow the girls are performing at this weekend. We'd love for you to come and watch."

"Come on, John!" the girls started calling out. "Please? Come!"

"Yeah. Sure. I think I can make it. But I better run. I'll see you guys there," I called over my shoulder, nodding at Santee and stuffing the flyer into my pocket.

I'd be lucky if I could walk tomorrow after the beating I'd be taking at practice.

*   *   *

I wasn't wrong. Unfortunately.

From the second I stepped onto the field, the coach was riding me. Hard.

"McCaffrey, do you have concrete in your shoes? Run!" he yelled.

"McCaffrey, are you going to let another one by you, or will you consider actually stopping one?" he shouted.

"Damn it, McCaffrey. Are you playing for our team or theirs? Because you're basically handing them the ball now," he shrieked.

"McCaffrey, have you slept at all? Are you getting enough rest, son? You look like you're falling asleep out there," he called across the field sarcastically.

Tanner ran past, laughing at me. "Come on, sleepyhead. Try to keep up," he sang over his shoulder. I stopped and bent over, hands on my knees, as I tried to catch my breath.

"McCaffrey!" the coach shouted at me.

I held up my hand.

"Are you holding your hand up at me, Boo-Boo?" Coach asked.

Boo-Boo? I shook my head, still trying to catch my breath. "No."

"Boys, I think what your teammate is trying to say is that you all need some extra laps...just to make sure you're getting enough exercise. Isn't that right, McCaffrey?"

I shook my head as the team groaned.

"Coach—" I began.

"So let's see you run, boys! Now!" The coach blew his whistle and stalked back toward the gym.

"Thanks a lot, John," Tanner said, banging into me with his shoulder as he ran past. "How about next time you try to actually show up on time?"

"Sorry, guys!" I called out. I rubbed my shoulder and started to run, catching up to Aiden and falling into step beside him. "Sorry," I said.

"It's fine," Aiden said. "If it wasn't you, it would be someone else making him mad."

Maybe, I thought. But I'd be a lot happier if it wasn't me for once.

Nine

My alarm rang shrilly right beside my head, shocking me out of a dream where I was taking a reality-TV star to prom. I jumped, reaching out and slamming it across the room. Oops.

It took me a minute to remember why I was getting up early on a Saturday morning when I didn't have school, soccer or dance. Then the promise I had made to Santee floated into my head, and I threw my legs over the side of the bed. I stood up, running a hand through my mop of hair. The Pow Wow.

I had never been to a Pow Wow that wasn't on my mom's reserve, and I didn't know what to expect. This one was in the city, so I figured there would be a lot more people. As I showered,

I considered the possibility that it would be much like dance class. And, much as I enjoyed learning with the girls and watching them dance, I wasn't sure I could handle an entire day of it. But a promise was a promise.

It was a forty-minute drive into the city, and I made it in record time. I pulled into the parking lot and watched as a steady stream of colorfully dressed people headed into the building. A rainbow array of blues, greens, reds and yellows paraded past. I was gratified to see as many adults as little kids walking in. I wandered in through the front doors and handed the usher my ticket. She directed me to the front row, where I found Santee bouncing in her seat.

"Hey!" She stood up and gave me a hug that nearly lifted me off my feet. "The girls will be so excited to see you! I was just about to give up on you."

"I told you I'd be here." I hugged her back.

"Well, have a seat. The Grand Entry is about to start, and I need to go line up with the girls."

"Yeah. Okay." I settled into my seat, wishing I had a coffee or something to wake me up a bit.

Santee rushed out of the row, apologizing and excusing herself as she stepped over the other spectators.

"Sorry," I said, shrugging at the woman next to me. "She's kind of excited." The woman nodded back and then turned to her program. "Ummm... have you been to many of these?" I asked her.

She glanced at me again. "Well, yes. My daughter, Moryah, dances." She pointed at a picture in her program of a beautiful girl staring fiercely into the camera while she danced. Her costume looked like it was on fire as it billowed around her.

"Wow!" I blurted out before I could stop myself. *Way to go, John.* I looked at the girl's mother, my face burning. "Sorry...I mean..."

She laughed. "It's okay. She's beautiful, isn't she?"

"Ummm...yeah." I pulled at my collar, which suddenly felt like it was choking me. The woman smiled kindly at me as the MC called out that the Grand Entry was beginning. The host drum started beating, and the voice of the lead singer rang out. Other voices joined in as the audience turned to the east end of the floor and watched the dancers start to move their feet to the drums and enter, one by one.

The people carrying the flags and Eagle Staffs entered first, followed by the elders. They danced in, feet moving in time to the drum. The men entered next. Grass dancers. Fancy dancers. Traditional dancers. Next came the women. Some wore shawls like the girls, and some wore bells. Some wore intricately beaded regalia. The teenagers came next. If I'd thought the colors of the people walking into the building were brilliant, seeing hundreds of them stepping to the sound of the drums under the bright lights of the arena was absolutely mind blowing. The Pow Wows back home were nothing like this.

"Whoa," I breathed. I had never seen anything like it. As I watched, the woman beside me waved excitedly at her stunning daughter. She was even more gorgeous when she smiled. I tore my gaze away from the girl as the junior dancers entered, and Taylor and the rest of the class danced their way onto the floor. They were tapping their feet and stepping lightly in time with the drums, led by a radiant Santee. She was definitely in her element, and I found myself wishing suddenly that I was down there with them.

Taylor looked up and beamed at me, waving enthusiastically and pointing me out to the other girls. Suddenly I had no less than a dozen giggling girls waving and calling out my name. I waved back, grinning at them and wishing again that I was down there dancing with them.

"Friends of yours?" the lady beside me asked.

"Something like that." I grinned, waving once more as the girls passed me. The Grand Entry was an amazing introduction to the incredible array of dancers and regalia. Some of them were young, like Taylor and the other girls, and some were older than my parents—but all were dressed in beautiful regalia and dancing proudly into the arena. After weeks of hiding from everyone and sneaking around to get to dance class, I saw the pride on the faces dancing past me and felt a sudden jolt of shame. I swallowed it, determined to enjoy the Pow Wow and not make it about myself or my own shortcomings.

There were several numbers I found myself enjoying more than I expected to before the girls took to the floor. I had seen their routine countless times, had even learned it right along with them. But seeing them with their hair braided, and clothed in their rainbow-hued regalia, made me so proud. Their intricately beaded shawls, skirts, shirts, leggings and vests were dazzling in shades of red, blue, yellow, pink, orange and green. They danced perfectly in sync until the very end, when Taylor had a thirty-second solo that had her spinning wildly, her braids whipping around her head. She ended the number with her signature leap through the air, and I was on my feet in an instant, clapping my hands with the rest of the audience. I stuck my fingers in my mouth and whistled. Taylor waved at me and curtsied with typical dramatic flair. I laughed and waved back as she turned and led the girls off the floor.

"They were wonderful!" the lady beside me said.

"I know!" I couldn't stop smiling. I was so proud of my classmates that I felt my eyes tear up. I blinked hard as the arena was plunged into sudden darkness and the drums boomed like thunder around me. As I tried to adjust my eyes to the dark, the lights flashed overhead like lightning, followed by another crash like thunder. The audience screamed and jumped, giggling at their reactions. I looked around, trying to see something as the lightning flashed again. I rubbed my eyes, then started as a spotlight flamed on, illuminating a lone dancer in the middle of the floor.

He stood still, staring out fiercely from a garishly painted face of black and white. He screamed out a war cry suddenly and ran across the arena as the drums crashed and then began to beat wildly. My heart pounded as the dancer ran right at me. I expected him to stop, but he kept coming. He ran at the barrier separating the arena floor from the first row of seats and took three steps up the wall directly in front of me before flipping over and landing back on the floor. My breath was taken away as I watched the man. He spun. He twirled. He leaped. He flipped. And every single second was absolutely exhilarating to watch.

The dancer dropped to one knee and pushed himself around in a circle with the other foot before leaping back to his feet. He again dropped to one knee, rose and dropped to the other knee. He stood and danced on, tipping one shoulder down, then the other. Then he spun on one foot, the other knee raised.

It was breathtaking, and like nothing I had ever seen. And it was over far too soon. The music ended with the warrior standing, arms in the air, face raised to the crowd, daring them not to applaud.

The entire crowd was on its feet. The ovation was deafening, and no one was louder than me. Santee was applauding beside me. I had no idea when she had even arrived.

"Did you see that?" I asked her.

"Isn't he amazing?" she responded.

"Yes!"

"Do you want to meet him?" she asked, smiling.

"Really?" I stared at her.

"Yeah, he's a friend of mine." She grabbed my arm. "Come on."

I followed her out of the row and through a door backstage, suddenly nervous. I saw the dancer at the end of the hall, talking to several other dancers in regalia.

Santee led me to him. "Great show as always, Sam," she said.

The man turned. "Santee!" He grabbed her in

a hug, lifting her feet off the floor and spinning her around. "Why weren't you dancing today?" he asked.

"My girls danced instead. I was with them for the Grand Entry though."

"Of course." In his happiness to see Santee, his face was completely transformed behind his makeup.

"Sam, I want you to meet a friend of mine. This is John McCaffrey. He just started dancing with me this year."

The dancer held out his hand. I couldn't reconcile this friendly guy with the fierce warrior I had just seen dancing as if his life depended on it. I shook hands with him, unable to think of a single thing to say.

"Hi, John. Did you enjoy the Pow Wow?"

"Yeah. Yes! It was amazing. You were...mind blowing!" I blurted out.

Sam clapped me on the back. "Thanks so much. I appreciate that." He took a swig from a bottle of water. "So you're a dancer?" he asked.

"No. Not really. I mean...I just started taking lessons with Santee and the girls. But I'm not a dancer. Not like you," I finished lamely.

"Don't listen to him," Santee interrupted. "John has a lot of potential."

"No...I mean, I'm trying, but..." I shrugged.

"I trust Santee's judgment. If she says you're a dancer, then you are."

I smiled shyly.

"Keep at it if it's something you love," he told me.

"I do!" I exclaimed. "I want to dance like you! I just..."

Sam raised an eyebrow and waited for me to continue.

I took a breath and decided to go for it. "Did your friends ever make fun of you? When you told them you were a dancer? And how did you juggle schoolwork and everything else?"

Sam smiled kindly and put a hand on my shoulder. "John, people will always find something to make fun of. People don't always understand. But if you truly love it, then you can't let them stop you from doing what you love. And if you want to be a dancer, don't let anything stand in your way. It's hard to juggle everything. I know that. You have to be strong enough to decide your own path, John. Does that make any sense?"

I nodded. "Yeah. It does. I mean, it's not easy sometimes. But when I hear the drums..."

"I know. You have to listen," Sam said. "So listen to them."

"I will," I promised.

People were calling Sam's name, and he glanced over, nodding at them. "I'm so sorry. I have to talk to them. Reporters," he said. "But it was great meeting you. I hope I see you in the Grand Entry next time."

"You will!" I told him, suddenly certain that he would. Sam waved and walked over to the reporters. I watched him posing for pictures and shaking hands and wanted, more than anything, to be just like him.

"So listen," Santee said, turning to me. "I've been wanting to talk to you about something."

"Yeah?" I asked, still watching Sam. There was just something about the guy that was so cool. Like he really knew who he was.

"You know that the girls and I love having you in class, right?"

"Sure."

"But I think you might learn more if you try dancing with your peers," she said.

"My peers? You guys are my peers," I told her.

Santee laughed. "Other boys, John. Remember when I told you that traditionally you'd learn by watching your elders dance?" I nodded. "Well, I think it would be good for you to learn from some other boys."

"Okay. But there isn't another class at the community center."

"I know. But Sam runs a group in the city that gets together every week to dance. The boys will all be around your age. I think you'd learn a lot."

"Wait...*that* Sam?" I pointed down the hall where the dancer was still talking to reporters.

"Yes." She nodded.

"I'd love to go!" Then reality struck. "But I don't think I can get to the city every week. I'd have to borrow the car. And I'm not sure if I could pay for the lessons."

"Okay. Well, I can't really help you with the car thing. But the Pow Wow group is through the Native Cultural Center. They don't charge anything."

"Even if my parents let me take the car, I'd still have to pay for gas. I have some money saved, but...I'll have to talk to my parents." I'd have to tell them about the dancing if I was going to drive into the city. And I had no idea what they'd say. I had no reason to think they would be anything less than supportive of anything I wanted to do. But I felt weird about telling them after keeping it a secret from everyone.

I looked over at Sam, who caught my eye and winked.

I wanted to dance like him. And if I had to come clean about dancing to my family, then so be it.

Ten

I was nervous, waiting for the perfect moment to tell my parents about dance class. I wasn't sure what my dad, who loved to watch sports and tinker with his car, would think of his son dancing. And since I had never shown the slightest interest in learning anything remotely traditional, I was worried my mom might think it was some kind of fad or something.

But I didn't want to lie to them anymore. Classes in the city would cut into my free time, and I couldn't expect to disappear with the car if I wasn't being honest with them.

I decided that dessert would be the best time to break the news of my new obsession with dance. My dad was full of roast beef and potatoes, and he patted his flat stomach, groaning happily at my mother.

"You've outdone yourself tonight. I'm stuffed!" he told her as she cleared his plate.

"Then I guess that apple pie will go to waste." She winked at him. They went through this routine every single time my mom made dessert.

"Apple? You didn't tell me it was apple! Just a small piece though. Not that small! A little bigger, please. Perfect. Thank you, my love." He sighed contentedly as my mother placed a huge wedge of apple pie down in front of him and topped it with a scoop of vanilla ice cream that immediately started to melt down the sides. "Mmm..."

My dad was happily savoring a giant mouthful of ice cream and pie. Now was definitely my moment.

"So I wanted to talk to you about something," I began. It was as good an opening as any, I supposed. My dad looked at me from behind his pie, and my mom sat down with a steaming cup of tea in her hand and blew on it, waiting for me to speak.

"What is it, nikosis?" she asked.

I took a deep breath and forged ahead.

"You know that I've been taking Jen to her art classes at the community center, right?"

My mother nodded.

"Well, the first time I took her, I was walking around the center, waiting for her to finish." I glanced up at my father, who had stopped eating and was watching me curiously. I swallowed, but he was looking at me so kindly—they both were—that I felt my nervousness melting away.

"I was bored, so I went exploring, and I heard the sound of drumbeats." I smiled, remembering how my heart had sped up when I saw Taylor and the girls. "I walked in and saw a bunch of girls dancing with shawls. And I wanted to try it too. *Not* with a shawl!" I quickly added, looking at my parents. "But that drum..." I trailed off, at a loss as to how to explain the way it had made me feel.

"It spoke to you," my mother finished, her face beaming.

"It did! I know it sounds ridiculous—"

"No, it doesn't," my mother interjected, reaching across the table and taking my hand.

"The drum is the heartbeat of Mother Earth. It's the heartbeat of our people."

I nodded.

"I've been dancing with them for a couple of weeks. I haven't told anyone yet. I wanted to try it out first, and I figured you wouldn't mind. I paid for the classes myself with the money I made cutting lawns. But I don't want my friends to know. I don't think they'd understand. And... I want to go to the Native Cultural Center in the city to dance with other guys my age. If it's okay with you."

"When is it?" my mother asked.

"It's on Saturday afternoons. And it won't cost anything but gas money. I have some saved. I can pay for that. I'd like to go, if it's okay." I looked from one of my parents to the other.

My father cleared his throat. "You can take my car." He stood, picked up his plate and walked toward the kitchen door, no doubt intending to finish his pie in front of the TV. He turned and looked fondly at my mother and then at me. "Don't worry about what anyone thinks, John. If you want to dance, then do it." He glanced at my mother again and nodded at her. "Remember who you are, son."

As he walked out of the kitchen, I looked at my mother. I was their son. Both of theirs. And I wanted to dance.

Eleven

There were flyers on a table inside the hallway of the Native Cultural Center, and since I was in no hurry to go in, I stopped and read one.

Long ago, when the world was much younger and much less complicated, the elders told stories about the first dancers. According to legend, the animals were the first dancers. It was the buffalo that swayed in their herds and the deer that leaped through the forest that showed our people how to dance.

I looked up as a couple of boys, laughing and shoving each other, walked past me and into the room where the dance group was meeting. I glanced at my watch. The class was about to start. I took a deep breath and followed them in.

As soon as I walked into the room, I felt the eyes of every single person there on me. It wasn't like the room full of little girls—these guys were my age. And, unlike me, they all looked like they belonged. I was well aware that I stood out like a sore thumb. I self-consciously put my bag on the floor and started stretching.

"Hey!" Sam walked over and held out a hand to me. "Nice to see you again! John, right?"

I nodded.

"I'm glad you came."

"Thanks." I took his hand and looked around at all the other boys, whispering and staring at me. "So you're the teacher?" I asked. I mean, clearly he was. But I literally couldn't think of one intelligent thing to say with all those kids staring at me.

He smiled kindly. "I just lead the group. Everyone is encouraged to go at their own pace and interpret the music in their own way. There aren't any tests or levels here. We're just here to dance and have fun. Find a spot and we'll get started."

I nodded and tried to calm the beating of my heart, which was so loud I was positive everyone in the room could hear it. I walked toward the back of the room and tried to look cool, nodding at the guy beside me as I took my place.

"Who the hell let the white kid in here?" I heard one of the boys say loudly enough for everyone but Sam to hear. My face colored.

"Dude, his face is as red as his hair."

If possible, I got even more flushed. The first guy who had spoken walked over to me. I looked desperately for Sam, but he'd stepped into the hall and was speaking on his phone.

I sighed. I was on my own with these jackals.

"Yep. I've got red hair. I know. Crazy, right?" I figured if I was in on the joke, they'd get tired of making fun of the new kid.

"What's wrong? Did you get tired of appropriating our culture for Halloween costumes and sports mascots?" he asked. "You figure you'll come in and take over our Pow Wows too?"

"What are you talking about?" I asked. "I'm not appropriating anything. I'm Aboriginal too." I waited for the skeptical response.

"Oh, right." He laughed, leaning heavily on the kid beside him, who was doubled over. "Let me guess. You're one-sixteenth Cherokee, right?"

"No. My mom..."

Sam walked in before I could finish, but frankly, it probably didn't matter. These guys already considered me the token white guy. You know...the white guy who wants to be Indigenous and hangs out at Pow Wows and wears beaded necklaces and a medicine pouch and stuff. Yep. Apparently, that was now me. Fantastic.

"Okay, everyone. Sorry for the delay. I hope you introduced yourself to our new friend, John." He turned to the men seated around the drum in the corner and nodded for them to start. Yeah. Did I mention they had live music?

The boys started dancing forward in a circle. I was immediately shut out of it as they closed rank.

"Jump in anywhere, John," Sam called out.

I nodded and pushed into the circle. One of the boys nudged me as I narrowly avoided stepping on his foot. "Sorry," I muttered. I stepped along in time to the music and was just getting into it when they stopped, causing me to slam into the kid in front of me.

"Watch it!" He scowled. "Jeez. White kids can*not* dance! Imagine seeing him tripping his way through the Grand Entry?" he said with a snort to the boy beside him.

I shook my head, trying to shrug him off. I turned toward the center and watched as one of the boys smoothly moved into it and began dancing by himself as the other boys looked on and waited for their own turns. The boy who had asked if I was one-sixteenth Cherokee was dancing fiercely, head bobbing and his feet tapping in time to the drum. He dropped to his knees and then flew back to his feet. I had no idea if any of these steps had actual names or if he was making it up as he went, but as I watched him spinning on one foot, I knew without a shadow of a doubt that there was absolutely no way I was going to dance in front of these guys.

Twelve

My life was basically an endless cycle of soccer practice, weight and cardio training with the team, school, a huge amount of homework, weekly dance classes and practicing on my own or with Santee whenever I could. I managed to grab something to eat once in a while and sleep for a few hours, but there were far too many nights when I fell asleep with my head resting on top of my schoolbooks. I knew I still wanted to dance, but being mocked in a Pow Wow group wasn't really in the plan. I had been going back and forth for days, wondering if I should bother returning to the Cultural Center or not.

As I laced up my cleats for soccer practice, I tried to leave all the stress behind and join in the usual banter with my teammates.

Aiden nudged me. "You okay?" he asked.

"What? Yeah. Yeah, I'm good. Ready to go!" I was a little overly enthusiastic, and I had to make a concerted effort to tone down a bit.

"McCaffrey!" The coach was yelling my name before he even turned the corner into the locker room. "You better be ready to run!" He stalked off to shout at someone else.

"Jeez. We haven't even started yet," I grumbled.

"Yeah, well...you've been a little distracted lately." Aiden held his hands up. "Sorry."

I nodded. I knew I hadn't been as focused as usual.

The coach stomped back into the room. "Are you going to sit around and chat all day? Or are you going to get up and run?"

The team ran drills and practiced taking shots on the goal, then passed the ball back and forth. I had run these drills so many times over the years that they were second nature by now. My mind wandered to the flyer I had read at the Cultural Center about the history of traditional dance, and I wondered for the millionth time if I should go back to Sam's dance group.

"Earth to McCaffrey!" the coach shouted.

"Right here, Coach!" I pulled my mind back to the soccer field.

"Dude, stop daydreaming," Aiden stage-whispered. "Coach is demented today."

"I know, I know. He's demented every day," I muttered under my breath, scowling. I fumbled the ball and tripped over my own feet.

"Oh, for crying out loud!" the coach yelled, blowing his whistle. "That's it. You can thank McCaffrey for this...thirty laps!" He blew his whistle again and walked away amid the groans of the team. My face burned.

"Thanks a lot, McCaffrey," Tanner called out as he jogged past me.

"Sorry," I mumbled. I turned to Aiden. "Did I really do anything *that* bad?" I asked as we started running side by side.

"Honestly? I don't think he's punishing you just for today," Aiden told me, speeding up a bit.

"What do you mean?" I asked, keeping pace.

"We both know that you haven't been focused for weeks. And the coach is taking it out on the rest of us," Aiden said.

"I know! But I'm doing my best." Frankly, I was getting tired of being ragged on all the time.

Aiden glanced over at me, his eyebrows raised. We ran the rest of the laps in silence.

The walk back to the locker room after practice was awkward. My teammates were grumbling around me about the extra laps, but most of the talk was good-natured. They had all had the coach's target on their backs at one time or another.

I was opening my locker when I felt a shoulder hit my back. Hard.

"Hey!" I turned around and met Tanner's angry gaze.

"Thanks again, McCaffrey. Really. We all appreciate the extra exercise," he said. "Maybe next time you can try to keep up with the rest of the team and not get us into trouble."

I opened my mouth to respond angrily but stopped. I glanced at Aiden, who was avoiding eye contact. I sighed. They couldn't all be wrong about my lack of focus, and I knew I was spreading myself way too thin.

"Yeah, sorry about that," I said.

Tanner looked surprised for a second but quickly recovered. "Yeah, you should be. If you don't want to be part of the team, there's the door," he told me.

I nodded. The best way to avoid conflict was to paste a grin on my face and nod. And figure out what the hell I really wanted to do.

Thirteen

I walked into the Native Cultural Center for my second Pow Wow class with my heart beating hard. I was hoping the whole "bust the new guy's balls" routine had worn off by now, but I was bracing myself just in case.

"Hey," I said to the guy nearest me when I walked in. I thought his name was Jasper. He nodded at me, and I felt myself relax a little. "Jasper, right?" I asked.

"Yeah." He started stretching beside me. Not much of a conversationalist apparently. Then he looked over at me. "And you're John?"

"Yes!" I smiled at him. Well, it was better than being taunted or ignored by all of them. "You're really good. Have you been dancing long?" I asked.

"Since I was a kid," he said.

"Jasper!" The guy who had insulted me the week before had just walked in. "Hanging with the white kid?"

"Nah. Just stretching, Matt," Jasper said, getting up and walking over to the bully and his cohorts.

Great. There goes the one nice guy.

"Dude, I can't believe you came back," Matt the bully said. "What's wrong? Didn't get enough last time?" He turned to his friends. "Man, I hate when people think they can hijack our culture like this." His buddies nodded in agreement. He turned to me. "Don't you have some Caucasian thing you could be doing? Like golf or something?"

His friends laughed. Including Jasper, I couldn't help but notice.

"Listen, I have just as much right to be here as you do," I began, but before I could finish, Sam walked in and called everyone to the center of the room.

How did I keep missing my chance to set these guys straight?

The drum started and I followed the other guys around, tapping my feet and trying to dance with my whole body.

"Dude!" Jasper whispered beside me, peering around—probably to see if anyone else heard him. "Grand Entry isn't about standing out."

"So what's it about?" I asked, but before he could answer, Sam had us form a circle where we'd keep tapping our feet lightly and each of us would get a chance to show off some fancy dance skills in the center.

I watched as Jasper danced into the middle of the circle. He was pretty awesome to watch. First he swayed his body as his feet kept up the steps we were all doing, a double tapping step around the circle. Suddenly he spun around in one direction, then switched the twirl the other way, arms outstretched and head bobbing to the drumbeats. His feet crossed over each other so quickly that I wondered how he managed not to trip over himself. I wanted to try that! He raised one knee high and spun around on one foot, then traded feet and spun the other way. The drumbeats stopped suddenly, and Jasper stopped with them, hands raised to the sky. The boys applauded as he left the circle.

"That was amazing," I told him.

He grinned breathlessly at me. "Thanks."

"Perfect, Jasper!" Sam called out. "Always remember that if you don't stop exactly when the drum stops, you'd be disqualified in competition."

Now *that* I didn't know. So how were you supposed to know when the drum was going to stop?

"John!"

I looked at Sam.

"Want to give it a try?" he asked.

"Umm...sure," I called back. I heard Matt snort behind me, but I held my head high. Like I had tried to tell him, I had just as much right to be there as he did. I moved into the center of the circle and listened as the drums began.

I tried to think of what Jasper had done and started swaying and moving my feet in time. I dipped my left shoulder down, then my right. So far, so good. I tapped a foot forward, then behind me. I switched legs and did the same before realizing with horror that I was doing the Lindy hop, that old 1920s dance. *Oh no!* I tried to cover it up by crossing my feet in front of each other and immediately got tangled. I fell. Hard. My elbow slammed against the floor, and I yelped in pain.

The boys howled with laughter until Sam reined them in.

"Come on, guys. John hasn't been dancing as long as the rest of you. You should be helping him along, not making fun of him." He walked over and reached down to help me up. "Are you okay?"

"Yeah," I said, rubbing my elbow, face burning. Did I really do the Lindy? How could I ever have thought this was the place for me? "Thanks," I told Sam. Then I turned around, picked my bag up off the floor and walked out.

Fourteen

I was quiet at dinner, which was fine because Jen kept up a steady stream of babbling conversation about art class and her friend Lia's dog, Daisy, who was "just so amazingly cute." I twirled strands of spaghetti on my fork, picturing myself twirling to the sound of the drum. I was tapping my fingers on the table and chewing when my mother called my name.

"John!"

"What? Sorry. I was thinking about something else." I smiled sheepishly.

"Yes. I can see that. You're a million miles away," my father said. My family was staring at me questioningly. Jen had even stopped talking and was shoving pasta into her mouth to make up for all the time she had lost in conversation. "Something wrong?"

"I don't know," I said, sighing. "I've just got a lot on my mind."

I saw my parents exchanging worried glances.

"Anything we can help with, honey?" my mother asked.

"Nah. Just school. And stuff. You know." I shrugged and tore my bread into chunks, mopping up my tomato sauce with it. I looked at the bread in my hand and then put it down on my plate without eating it, my appetite gone. I looked at my parents. "Have you ever had anyone judge you for how you look?"

My father nodded thoughtfully. "I got made fun of a lot in school because of my red hair. It's probably not the same now, but back in the day, they laughed at me. Called me Little Orphan Annie or Ronald McDonald. Little Red Riding Head. Even my friends called me Red or Ginger. Kids would chant at me, *I'd rather be dead than have red on my head.* I hated that one. Or *Red, Red, pee your bed, wipe it up with gingerbread.*" He looked over at me. "Is that what you mean?"

"Umm. Not exactly. They really said that stuff?" Wow. Kids were mean back in my father's day.

"That and worse," he admitted.

What could possibly be worse than that one about wiping your pee up with gingerbread? I wondered. I probably didn't want to know.

"The kids sometimes make fun of me," my sister interjected.

I hadn't even been aware that she was listening. "They do?" I asked.

"Yeah. It doesn't bother me, mostly. But I don't like when they call me things."

"What do they call you?" my mother asked.

"I had a teacher call me 'that Indian girl' once," she admitted, not meeting anyone's eyes and pulling on the ends of her braids.

"What?" my father asked, his eyes wide.

"Yeah. He was a substitute. And there was a girl before who didn't like me. She told everyone that I was dirty. She said all Indians were dirty. I told her that was stupid."

"Someone actually said that to you?" I was astonished. The truth was, I'd never faced anything like this. I might be half Cree, but I didn't look it at all. Which was, ironically, a bit of a problem for me right now. But my sister's issue was much more serious. She was only eleven and clearly dealing with racism.

"Did you know about this?" I asked my parents.

"We knew about the girl," my father answered, sighing. "But we hadn't heard about the teacher."

"Well, I'm sorry you have to deal with that," I blurted out. I felt like I should have been protecting her somehow.

She shrugged. "It's okay. Mom and Dad talked to me about it years ago. They told me people might say mean things to me but that I had to be strong and not let them get to me. That we're better than that." She beamed at my mom, who patted her hand and looked at my father.

"Why didn't you have that conversation with me?" I asked.

"We didn't think you'd have the same thing happen to you," my father admitted.

"But we should have talked to you too. I'm sorry," my mother finished. "So what is happening with you?"

How could I possibly complain that the guys at the Pow Wow group didn't think I was Aboriginal after Jen's confession?

"Nothing. It was nothing."

Fifteen

I walked into the class and waited to be noticed. It didn't take long.

"John!" Taylor screamed, running and jumping on me. I managed to keep my balance. Barely. The other girls turned at her shriek and ran over to hug me. Santee looked at me questioningly, then grinned and walked over.

"What on earth are you doing here?" she asked, hugging me.

"I missed you guys!" I said, trying to untangle myself from the pile of girls crowding around me. "I thought maybe I could come back here and dance with you guys."

"Yeah!" the girls yelled, jumping up and down.

Santee frowned at me, clearly wanting to ask me more questions, but she called the girls over.

"So since our friend John has come to visit, maybe he can show us what he's learned in his classes at the Native Cultural Center," she said. The girls cheered, and Santee picked up her remote to turn on the CD player. "So?" she asked me, nodding toward the floor.

I took a deep breath and walked into the center of the floor. She hit *Play* and the room filled with the sound of drumbeats. And just like that, I was home.

Without the specter of Matt and the rest of the guys at the Cultural Center standing around and watching, I danced. No one laughed at me as I spun and bobbed my head in time to the drums. No Lindy hop this time. I raised one arm in the air and lowered my other shoulder, then danced around in a circle on one foot, then switched arms and changed directions. I dropped down to one knee, then leaped back up. I dropped to the other knee and rose again. I imagined myself in elaborate regalia and crossed my arms back and forth in front of myself as if I were holding whip sticks and spun and spun and spun.

For the first time since I'd started the classes in the city, I felt joy again as I danced. These girls wouldn't care if I missed a step or lost my balance. If I was awkward, I wouldn't be judged here. It was a huge relief to just breathe and dance. I listened to the music and pulled one knee up high, spinning on one foot one way, then the other, until I heard the last honor beats—the loud beats interspersed throughout the song that signal dancers to honor the drum. I came to a stop on the last drumbeat with my legs spread, knees bent and my arms up in the air.

I had literally *never* managed to stop on the last beat before! Santee and the girls applauded madly.

"Great job, John!" Santee called out, beaming at me. "Looks like the classes with the boys have been good for you!"

"Yeah," I said, breathing hard.

I didn't know how to begin telling her what the classes in the city had really been like, but I finally got my chance when the girls were filing out after class.

"That was an amazing performance today, John," Santee told me, gathering up her things and getting ready to leave.

"Yeah. About that," I began. She looked at me, eyebrows raised. "I thought maybe I could come back and dance with you guys again."

"Why?" Santee asked. "You're obviously doing great with Sam and his group."

"Umm...I just...I don't think I'm fitting in there." I didn't meet her eyes as I said this.

"Did something happen with one of the boys?" she asked.

I sighed deeply. "Not one of them, no."

"So then, what is it?"

"It's all of them! They treat me like I have no right to be there. They call me 'that white kid' and I'm a total klutz in front of them!"

"Wow." Santee let out a deep breath. "What did Sam say?"

"He doesn't know," I admitted. "They don't do it when he's there. I keep trying to tell them who I am...who my mother is...but they don't give me the chance. They assume because I don't look like them that I'm an outsider. I can't dance with them," I finished, finally looking at her.

Her face looked sympathetic. "I'm sorry. They shouldn't be making you feel that way. You're welcome to come and dance with us, John. But even in the short time you've been with Sam, you've come so far with your dancing. Just by watching them."

I nodded. "Yeah. They're really good. I've been trying some of their moves and changing others a bit to make them my own, you know?"

Santee looked thoughtfully at me before answering. "You can't get that with us. So you have to decide what you want to do. You can dance with us and stay at the same level. Or you can watch boys who have been dancing since they were kids and really learn something. What is it you want out of this?" she asked.

I thought for a moment. "I'd really like to be in the Grand Entry, like you and the girls were. And I think maybe...maybe I'd like to try to compete someday."

"Then what do you need to do?"

"I need to go back to Sam's group," I admitted.

Santee hugged me. "Come on," she said, sliding an arm through mine. "I'll walk you to your car. And for the record, there's a Pow Wow coming up in about a month, if you think you'll be ready for the Grand Entry."

As I got into my car, I felt better than I had in a while. I hadn't solved my problem with the guys at the Cultural Center, but Santee had pointed out how far I had come just by watching them and learning from them.

I turned to put my backpack on the passenger seat and looked at the gym bag I had left there. I felt like a bucket of ice water had been poured over me.

I had completely forgotten about soccer practice.

Sixteen

I was still feeling good about the decision I had made to go back to the Cultural Center and stand up for myself when I arrived at school the next morning. Confronting Matt might not immediately solve all my problems with him, but it was a start.

I was mentally going over my math homework when someone shoved me into a locker.

"Hey!" I turned and stared into the angry faces of several of my teammates, led by Tanner. "Oh," I said. Frankly, I knew they had every reason to be upset with me.

"Yeah. *Oh.*" Tanner crossed his arms over his chest, his biceps bulging. "Where the hell were you yesterday, McCaffrey?" he asked.

"I...uh...had a medical appointment," I answered lamely.

"Right. Well, while you were off playing doctor the rest of us were working our asses off." My teammates laughed, and I tried to join in and show I was a good sport. Tanner glared down at me. "Listen, McCaffrey, we don't need you anymore. The team is doing just fine without you."

"Lay off, Tanner," Aiden called out, walking up beside me.

"Are you kidding me? You're really going to stand up for this loser?"

Aiden nodded. "Yeah, I am. He's still part of our team."

"Oh yeah? Well, tell your girlfriend that he better start acting like it." Tanner turned and stalked off down the hallway, closely followed by the other soccer players.

I turned to Aiden.

"Thanks," I said, nodding at my friend.

"Don't mention it," Aiden replied. "Just...don't make me do it again, John. Get back in the game."

I nodded my thanks, but I wasn't entirely sure if I could do that. I finally knew where my heart was leading me. And it wasn't onto the soccer field. Or to Santee's class.

Seventeen

had agreed to meet Santee again after school. It wasn't a regular class day, but she said she'd have a surprise waiting for me. I didn't know what to expect, so I was a little nervous when I dropped Jen off at her art class and made my way through the community center to the gymnasium. It was quieter than usual in the hallway without the echo of the drumbeats and the pounding of feet keeping time.

I opened the gym door and walked in, glancing across the room. Santee was standing in the middle of the floor, smoothing the feathers of the most incredible regalia I had ever seen. I stopped dead and stared, my mouth falling open. Was that for me?

It was blue and orange. It was beaded and feathered, with moccasins, a headband and cuffs. The shirt and pants and apron were elaborately embroidered and beaded. Every single piece was breathtaking, but the two feather bustles, one to be worn around my neck and one around my waist, with matching bustles for my arms... I could already picture them moving in time to the music. It was an outfit that had to be seen to be believed.

"Is that really for me?" I asked, unable to take my eyes off of it.

Santee laughed. "You bet it is. Want to try it on?"

I was almost afraid to touch it. It looked fierce and delicate at the same time. But I was dying to put it on, and I was even more eager to dance in it. I remembered how the dancers at the Pow Wow looked all dressed up. I thought about Sam in his regalia. They looked like warriors. And I wanted more than anything to be one of them.

"I do...but I'm not sure I know how to get into it," I confessed sheepishly.

"Just get the pants and shirt on, and I'll help with the rest," Santee said.

That much was easy. I changed quickly behind the curtain onstage and stepped out. It fit like a glove so far. I sat on the edge of the stage and pulled the moccasins on.

"How did you know what size I wear?" I asked her.

"Taylor checked your clothes tags for me." She winked. "Jump down so I can get all of this on you."

I dropped to the floor and walked over to her. I already felt different. Stronger. I stood tall as she helped me tie on fur anklets and bells. She showed me how to put on the front and back aprons and the beaded side tabs. She dressed me in my belt and cape and tied a harness around my neck, my arms spread out to the side.

My favorite part was the roach. It was a stunning headdress and, according to Santee, was made of deer hair and porcupine guard hair. It was set on something called a rocker, which would do exactly what its name implied. It would make the headdress rock and dance when I moved my head. Santee got the roach ready but put it aside so she could get the bustles on me.

The bustles were circles of feathers. One went on my back and one around my waist. There were two smaller ones for my arms. Once Santee had those in place, she tied on an intricately beaded headband, followed by my roach. She handed me two whip sticks that I gave a practice twirl to, just to see them dance.

Santee stood back and looked me up and down, an expression I took to be pride spreading over her face.

"Perfect. I brought a mirror." She gestured to where she had a full-length mirror leaning against the wall. "Take a look."

As I walked toward the mirror, bells jingled lightly and feathers shook around me. I looked at the mirror as I got closer and saw the reflection of a man, a dancer and a warrior walking forward.

"That's not me," I said.

Santee walked up behind me and straightened the cuff on my arm. "Yes, it is. You look incredible."

"I thought it would feel heavy and weigh me down. But it's light. I feel like...I feel like I can fly," I told her, meeting her eyes in the mirror.

Santee started the music and sat down against the wall. "Show me," she told me.

I closed my eyes for a moment and then started to dance. Somehow, with my new regalia on, I could twirl faster, jump higher and hear the music in ways I never had before. I didn't just fly—I soared. Without giving it a thought, I did a move I had only seen on a TV movie about kids who did capoeira. I jumped down sideways like I was going to do a cartwheel but threw my feet up and held all my weight on one hand for a moment. Santee burst into applause, but I kept dancing. I balanced on one foot, my other knee high in front of me, and spun around and around. First one way on my right foot, then the other way on my left. I tapped my feet and shook my shoulders, making the feathers wave madly around me. I knew this music, so I knew when to stop suddenly, ending the dance with the last drumbeat. I stood still, chest heaving as I tried to catch my breath.

Santee was on her feet, cheering wildly. She ran across the room and threw her arms around me and hugged me tightly. "That was brilliant!" she told me. "How did you feel?"

"Like a warrior," I replied.

Santee led me to a chair and handed me a bottle of water, which I gulped gratefully. She started going over her notes and I listened, nodding or adding my own thoughts here and there. I saw the curtain onstage rustle out of the corner of my eye, but I chose to ignore it, figuring someone must have opened the door to the hall for some reason, and continued my conversation with Santee.

It was a decision I was about to regret.

Eighteen

I knew something was up as soon as I walked into the school the next day. There was a buzz in the air. I wondered what everyone was talking about as I started walking to my locker. I saw a group of senior girls looking down at a phone and giggling. I passed a couple of juniors who looked up from another phone and stared at me. The farther down the hall I got, the more people seemed to be looking at me and laughing or whispering together. At first I ignored it... but the closer I got to my locker, the clearer it became that everyone was talking about me. I tried to ignore the whispers and laughter, but the fact that people were openly staring at me was a little harder to ignore.

"John?" Aiden had walked up behind me.

"Hey," I said, relieved to see a friendly face.

Aiden didn't smile back. "You need to see something," he told me.

"What?" I asked, my heart pounding. This couldn't be good.

Aiden handed me his iPhone without a word. I took it and glanced down at the screen. *Oh no.*

Aiden had already hit *Play*, and I saw a video of myself dancing around the gymnasium in my regalia, with a huge grin on my face. I heard a loud bray of laughter across the hall and looked up to see a group of kids glancing back and forth between their phones and me. I felt the heat creeping up the back of my neck as my face slowly colored.

I pushed the phone back at Aiden. "Where did you get this?" I asked, my voice low.

"It got sent to the whole soccer team."

"By who?" I asked, even though I already had a pretty good idea who had done this.

Aiden paused. "Tanner," he said.

"And now everyone's seen it?" I asked.

Aiden nodded. "Yeah. Pretty much. It's been forwarded a lot. And it's on YouTube."

I closed my eyes, taking deep breaths, willing myself to calm down.

"Why didn't you tell me?" Aiden's voice brought me back. "We've been friends since second grade. You could have told me why you've been missing soccer."

I looked at him, surprised. "I didn't tell anyone, Aiden. Look how they're all laughing at me!" I gestured around the hall.

"Yeah, well...I wouldn't have laughed," Aiden said.

"Okay. I'm sorry, all right? I am."

Aiden nodded.

"Now, where the hell is Tanner?" I asked, looking down the hall toward the locker room.

Nineteen

I shoved the locker-room door open and stalked past rows of lockers, Aiden following close behind, until I found Tanner. He was lying on his back on a bench with a couple of our teammates sprawled out around him. I came to a dead stop and watched everyone turn to look at me. They all looked away guiltily. My so-called friends.

Tanner was the only one who met my eyes. He propped himself up on one elbow and looked at me with a smirk spreading slowly across his face. "Well, hello, princess."

Before I had a chance to think it through, I stepped forward and grabbed one end of the bench that Tanner was lying on and wrenched it high off the floor, sending him sliding hard off the other end.

He landed in a tangled pile of limbs on the floor and looked up at me in complete shock. "What the hell do you think—"

"Shut up! Why, Tanner? Why would you spy on me? And why would you send that video to everyone on the team? You knew it would get shared and posted and tagged. How could you do that to me? I thought we were friends." I was standing over him.

Tanner looked up at me. "Hey, it was just a joke."

"A joke? That was private!"

"Yeah," Tanner said. "I can see why. Lighten up, McCaffrey. No one cares if you want to prance around in a dress in your free time."

Before I could react, Tanner dove forward and grabbed me around the waist, bringing me down with him. The other boys ran out of the room, shouting for the coach as I threw a punch that caught Tanner in the right eye. Aiden ran forward and tried to pull us apart, yelling for us to stop as Tanner punched me in the mouth. I ducked to avoid being hit again as the coach ran into the locker room, followed by the rest of the boys. He grabbed Tanner while Aiden pulled me off him.

"Enough!" the coach roared. "What is going on here?"

I spit a mouthful of blood onto the floor and wiped my swollen lip, glaring at Tanner. Tanner stared back at me through his one good eye, the other already swollen completely shut and turning purple.

"You're both done for the day. Go home. Clean up. I don't want either of you on my field today." The coach turned to leave, then walked back to us, the anger gone from his face. "And McCaffrey? Figure out where your loyalties lie, okay? You're letting your teammates down. If you can't be there for them, you need to walk away."

I nodded, touching my swollen lip.

"Go home and put some ice on that. You too, Tanner." The coach left the now dead-silent locker room.

"You okay?" Aiden asked me.

"Yeah. You better get to class," I told him, walking to the door.

I had no idea how I was going to explain this to my parents.

Twenty

My parents stared at me as I held an ice pack to my mouth while it throbbed in time with my heartbeat.

"So why did this boy hit you?" my mother asked, looking perplexed.

I shrugged. "I haven't been pulling my weight with the team. I missed a couple of practices because I was dancing. I guess I just pushed him too far. I got mad, and a couple of punches were thrown. It was nothing. Just guy stuff."

"But why didn't the principal call us if you got sent home?" she asked.

"He doesn't know about it. Coach sent us both home to cool off. Everything is fine. I'm not even in trouble."

My mother clucked around me and refilled my ice pack while my father looked at me thoughtfully. Mom announced that she was going to make a poultice to help with the swelling and bruising, then went out to her garden. As soon as we were alone, my father leaned in to talk to me. Man to man.

"It's not like you to fight, son," he said quietly. "Is there anything you want to talk about?"

I shrugged as if it was no big deal. "Tanner took a video of me dancing and sent it to the entire soccer team. He spied on me, and now it's up on YouTube."

"Ah. And everyone knows about the dancing now," he said, his face sympathetic.

"Yeah. The video got sent around to the entire school."

"Okay. So the secret's out."

"Yeah. It is," I said, probing my swollen lip with the tip of my tongue.

"Then you don't have to hide it from anyone anymore, right?"

"I guess not," I admitted.

"Then, misguided as it was, he did you a favor."

I stared at him. "What do you mean? He spied on me and humiliated me!"

"Yes. But now they all know." He took a sip of his coffee. "A secret like that is hard to keep, son. It eats away at you when you have to hide something from your friends. Especially when it's something you love that you're hiding."

"But they were all laughing at me."

"And tomorrow they'll find something else to laugh at. You hid it like you had something to be ashamed of," he said. "You don't. You should be proud of your heritage, John. Remember who you are and hold your head up." He patted my shoulder and grabbed his coffee mug. "Gonna get a refill," he said, standing up.

"Okay, Dad." I watched my father's retreating back and thought about how cool my parents actually were.

Twenty-One

I spent much of the night tossing and turning. My mouth was still swollen, and it throbbed steadily. I touched it with the tip of my tongue for the hundredth time, then flopped over onto my side and pulled the blankets off with me. It was no use. I might as well get up, early as it was. There was no way I was getting any sleep anyway.

I glanced at my alarm clock. Five in the morning. And it was still dark outside. But I needed time to figure out what I was going to say to the team, and I couldn't do that without a pot of coffee and maybe a bowl of cereal. I threw my legs over the side of the bed and sat up, yawning and stretching. My body had finally gotten used to the abuse it suffered at dance class, and I felt stronger and more agile. I stood up and padded down the hall and into the kitchen to start a pot of coffee and find something to eat. It was quiet at this hour. My sister and parents were still asleep, and as I sat down at the kitchen table and looked out the window at the maple tree in the backyard, I felt peaceful for the first time in weeks.

When the coffee was ready, I poured myself a cup and blew on it. I put my feet up on the table, something my mother would have heartily disapproved of if she had been awake to see it. I sipped and felt the coffee burn my tongue slightly as I swallowed. I looked at the clock. Five thirty. Still an hour and a half until soccer practice. I could be in the gym by six and have an hour to do some strength training and figure out what I was going to say to everyone.

It was still quiet when I got to the weight room. I knew people would start trickling in soon, and I wanted to get a few reps in before they did. I settled on a bench and got to work.

"Need a spotter?" a voice called out near the door. I looked up in mid-chest press and saw Aiden walking into the room.

"Yeah! Come grab this, would you?"

Aiden walked over and helped lift the bar. "Come on. I think you've got another couple in you. Let's go! Push it out!"

I grunted but pushed out two more chest presses.

Aiden helped me rack the weight bar. "Good job, buddy."

"Thanks. We've got half an hour before practice. You can have the bench. I need to do some legs." I stood up and wiped my face with a towel, grabbing my water bottle and taking a long drink.

Aiden sat down on the bench. "Spot me?" he asked. I nodded and stood behind him, helping guide the bar as Aiden started to lower the weight. "So...you're here. Does that mean you're still on the team?"

"Yeah. I am. If you guys will still have me. I think I owe everyone an apology first though," I admitted.

Aiden racked the weight bar and sat up. "Well, you're about to get your chance."

I glanced over at the clock. Quarter to seven. We had to grab our gear and get onto the field before the coach got there.

* * *

I walked into the locker room, followed closely by Aiden. The last time I had been in there, Tanner and I had gotten into a fight. I saw Tanner standing by his locker, surrounded by the other guys who had been with him at the fight. He stood up straighter and whispered something to his friends, who turned toward me. They all knew about the fight, so they were looking between Tanner and me, waiting to see what was going to happen. They were either expecting another brawl, or hoping for one.

I headed straight over to Tanner and stood in front of him, Aiden still a step behind me. Tanner looked at me, waiting for me to speak but ready to throw a punch, if his clenched fists were any indication.

I took a deep breath and held out my hand. Tanner stared at it for a second, clearly surprised. He looked at me quizzically. I nodded, still holding out my hand. Tanner reached out tentatively, and I took his hand and shook it. Aiden let out a sigh of relief behind me.

I let go of Tanner's hand and spoke loud enough for everyone in the room to hear me. "Tanner, I owe you an apology." I turned to look at my teammates. "I owe all of you an apology. And that's not easy for me. But in dance, they train you to be a warrior. And a warrior would own up to his mistakes. I let all of you down, and I'm truly sorry for that. I can't quit dancing. But I can make sure that I'm here to train with you guys and to give 100 percent in every game." I looked at Tanner again, then around the room. "If you'll let me."

"It's okay with me," Aiden called out.

"Me too," one of my teammates called out, followed by others adding their own comments.

I looked at Tanner. "Well?" I asked. "What do you say?"

Tanner could be an idiot, but to his credit he actually looked around the room to gauge what the team wanted before he answered.

"I guess you can have another chance. But if you screw it up or let us down in any way, I'll give *you* a black eye."

I nodded at him. "Fair enough."

"Then let's get on the field before Coach makes us run laps again," Aiden said.

It was a strenuous practice, but for the first time in ages, I was fully present. I had made things right with the team, and I was eager to show them that I meant what I'd said. I ran up and down the field. I passed the ball with pinpoint accuracy. And I made an absolutely stunning save when I dove in front of the net, arching my back and kicking a foot up above my head to send the ball flying back down the field.

"Dude! Nice save!" Aiden yelled out, slapping me on the back as he ran past.

"Nice move, McCaffrey," Tanner called over his shoulder.

"Thanks. Maybe those dance classes improved my game," I joked.

The team was completely in sync, and the coach was actually smiling and yelled much less than usual. "Good practice, boys. Keep that up and we'll be unbeatable. Hit the showers, everyone."

I fell into step beside Aiden and started for the school, congratulating him on a particularly great play.

"McCaffrey, stay back a second," the coach called.

I stopped, and Aiden raised an eyebrow at me. "See you later," he said before jogging off to the showers.

"Yeah," I muttered. I turned around. "What's up, Coach?"

"Listen, I just wanted to tell you that a lot of professional athletes take dance classes."

I looked at him in shock. Of all the things he could have told me, this was the last thing I expected.

"They...what? Really?" I asked.

The coach nodded. "Yeah. They do. It helps with coordination and agility. Even helps build strength. Ever hear of Lynn Swann?" he asked.

"Uh, I don't think so. Who's she?"

"She? Oh dear Lord. Lynn Swann! *He* used to play for the Steelers?"

I shook my head.

"They called him The Baryshnikov of Football! He took dance classes to help him on the field."

"Did it work?" I asked.

"Yeah, it did. And it's helping you too. You're more confident out there, McCaffrey. And I can see a difference in your game too." He shrugged. "Anyway. I just wanted you to know that. Go hit the showers," he called over his shoulder as he walked away.

I stared after him wordlessly. My dad was right. Tanner *had* done me a favor. I had forgotten who I was and that I should be proud of my culture. Both sides of it. And it was time I stood up to the boys at the Cultural Center.

Twenty-Two

I had a plan.

Santee was right. I had learned a lot from the boys at the Cultural Center, and if I wanted to dance, I needed to find a way to go back and fit in. I knew I belonged there, but I needed them to know it too, or I'd never feel comfortable. I had to prove I could dance as well as the rest of them. And to do that, I needed some help.

I needed my family.

*   *   *

I got home fifteen minutes before my mom came in with Jen, and twenty minutes before my dad got there. I was already in the kitchen, dicing tomatoes and slicing cucumbers for a salad by the time Jen ran in, looking for a snack.

I rapped her knuckles with the dull edge of the knife when she reached for a cucumber slice.

"Hey!" She rubbed her fingers and pouted.

"Those are for the salad."

She gave me her patented puppy-dog eyes—they really were pretty impressive—until I gave in and passed her a chunk of cucumber.

She smirked at me and bit into it. "What's up with you making dinner all of a sudden?"

I shrugged. My mom walked in, carrying pizza. The smell of cheese and pepperoni made my mouth flood with saliva.

"Are you making a salad?" she asked, stopping to put the pizza down on the counter.

"Don't everyone act so surprised. I just thought I should help out since I'm actually home on time."

"Well, I, for one, appreciate the gesture." My mother kissed me on the cheek.

My father walked in and looked at me. "Are you making salad?" he asked.

"Oh, come on!" I threw the veggies on top of the lettuce I had already torn up into a bowl as Jen started laughing.

I carried it out to the dining-room table and sat down with my family. We all dug into the pizza and scooped salad onto our plates. I waited until everyone was on their second slice before I brought up my plan.

"So...you know how I've been going to the Cultural Center in the city?"

"Of course," my mother said, chewing on her pizza.

"Well, as I told Dad"—I nodded toward my father—"I've been having trouble fitting in."

My mother frowned.

"Some of the boys have been making comments and saying I don't belong because I'm white."

"That's ridiculous!" my mother exclaimed.

"They don't know anything about me, Mom. They're just going by what I look like. Kinda like what happens to Jen sometimes, I guess." I looked at my sister, and she nodded back at me. "I haven't been able to dance well. I guess I've been feeling insecure or something. I haven't stood up for myself, and I need to do something about that. I know that I deserve to be there too. I want to do something to prove it. To make an impression," I finished.

My parents looked at me expectantly while Jen picked all the pepperoni off a slice of pizza and added it to a piece already smothered in pepperoni.

"That's where you come in, Jen." I watched as she looked up, surprised to be included.

"Me?" she asked, incredulous.

"Yeah, you. You're the only one who can help me with this part. I'll need all of you there at the next class. But Jen, I need you to help me get ready for it."

"How?" she asked. "What can I do?"

"You took gymnastics for years," I said. "You even went to gymnastics camp, right?"

"Yeah. So?"

"So I need to learn some tricks. Can you teach me a backflip?" I asked.

Jen grinned widely. "You bet I can," she said and high-fived me.

Twenty-Three

Jen took me out into the backyard, climbed up onto our trampoline and started to jump.

"Hey! I thought we were going to work on my backflip," I said.

"We are," Jen said, jumping higher.

"How?" I asked.

She took one last big jump and flew into the air, then executed a perfect backflip before she landed on her feet again.

"Whoa!" I clapped my hands. "That was amazing! Do it again!"

Jen grinned and pumped her arms to get higher, bending her knees and then throwing herself backward again.

"All right, Supergirl. Let me give it a try."

Jen came to a stop and helped me climb onto the trampoline. She moved to the edge as I started jumping in the middle of the trampoline.

"Wait, wait, wait! Stop!" she yelled.

I stopped jumping and stared at her, puzzled. "What?"

"You don't start with jumping! You have to start by just standing still," she said.

"What? Why?" I asked.

"Because I said so," she replied sternly. "Now stand still."

I nodded, raising my eyebrows at her. "Yes, ma'am."

"Stand right in the middle," she told me. "Feet shoulder-width apart. Good. Now put your arms above your head. Look straight ahead. Pick something to focus on."

I followed her instructions. "Got it."

"Good. Now bend your knees a bit. That's too much! Better. Now swing your arms hard. That's what's going to give you enough momentum to do the flip. Harder! Don't bend your elbows though."

I stopped for a minute. "That's a lot to remember."

"Yeah, well, we're just starting. Now focus!"

I nodded and started swinging my arms again and bending my legs. I had to admit, I felt a little silly, but Jen had been taking gymnastics and coaching kids younger than her for years. I had to trust her.

"Now, you don't want to jump back...you want to jump up, okay?"

"Why?"

"Because I said so!" I raised an eyebrow at her. "Because you'll lose your balance. Trust me. So just jump up—and you want to tuck your knees up. Good! That's perfect. Keep doing that. Great."

I jumped and did tucks for a while. I had this part down. "Now what?" I called.

"If you're ready to try it, you're going to tighten your muscles—your abs and your legs. And don't throw yourself backward with your arms. You want to use your hips. Pivot back. I'll spot you."

Jen moved into the center of the trampoline while I stood still and tried to put it all together in my head.

"How are you going to spot me? I weigh twice what you weigh."

"More, probably," she said. "But my counselor at gymnastics camp weighed more than you, and I spotted him. I'm just going to put one arm behind you and one in front, and I'll help you over. Ready to try it?" she asked.

I nodded and practiced swinging my arms around and bending my knees.

"Okay. So just do a big jump and pivot?" I asked.

"That's it. I'll help get your legs over."

"Are you sure about this?" I looked at her, concerned I was about to break my leg. Or, worse, my neck.

"Trust me. I know what I'm doing. I swear." She crossed her heart solemnly.

I laughed. "All right, let's do this."

"Yes!" Jen clapped her hands and got into position beside me. "Wait!"

I was about to jump but stumbled to a stop. "What?"

Jen moved to the side again. "Sorry. But why don't you just jump and land on your back a couple of times? I forgot that step. Sometimes it helps to know that you're not going to get hurt."

I nodded thoughtfully. It made sense. I jumped a few times and then threw myself backward. I tensed up the first time, but the next two times I landed easily.

"Okay. I've got it. Let's try the flip."

"All right. Go for it!" Jen was back in position, ready to spot.

I looked ahead and bent my knees. I gathered myself...concentrated...and then jumped. As I flew into the air, I tensed up and pivoted my hips forward, tucking my knees into my chest and sending myself backward. I felt Jen's hands on me, helping me flip backward. I landed on my butt and bounced hard.

"I did it!" I yelled, jumping up and hugging her.

She hugged me back. "Almost. Try to land on your feet this time. I don't think the judges are going to be too impressed if you land on your butt."

"Funny." I stuck my tongue out at her. "Come on. Let's try again."

"Do you really think you can do a backflip in your costume?" she asked.

"Regalia," I told her. She looked at me blankly. "That's what the costumes are called." I paused. "I think so. Eventually. I saw dancers online doing it, so I know it can be done. But let's just focus on me learning how to do it in normal clothes for now. That's all I really need to know how to do when I go back to the Cultural Center."

"All right. Then let's try again."

It took another hour before I could land a backflip without Jen spotting me and without the crash landing. I high-fived her, utterly exhausted.

"You are one amazing coach," I said, panting as I lay on the trampoline.

"Told you so." She tossed her hair over her shoulder, smirking at my obvious discomfort. "Now we just have to get you to do it on the ground."

I groaned.

Twenty-Four

J en had become my sidekick for the week.
I was used to her being a pesky little sister,
but having her as a backflip coach and cheer-
leader was amazing. She celebrated with me
when I landed a perfect backflip on the grass in
the backyard, she did her homework in the gym
while I practiced my routine, and she gave me
constructive criticism in the car.

"You've got that great capoeira move, but
you're still stumbling slightly when you land
back on your feet," she told me as we drove back
from the community center.

The glowing orange globe of the sun was
slowly sinking in front of us. I was exhausted,
and everything hurt, but I still didn't have the
routine down.

"I know," I said. "It's the corkscrew move right after. Where I spin downward? It throws me off balance because all my weight is on one side."

"Okay, then you have to compensate for it. You'll have to pivot your hips again. Like in the backflip. Maybe move into a few crow steps? Instead of just throwing your weight back to land on your feet, tighten your muscles and pivot into the crow step."

"Yeah, that's a really good idea, Jen!" I told her. "I'll definitely try that."

* * *

I had a soccer game that evening, and all the gymnastics and jumping on the trampoline had definitely improved my balance and stamina. The muscles in my legs flexed as I ran up and down the field, passing the ball deftly to my teammates. I headed toward the goal and caught a pass that Tanner sent straight to me. I weaved around a player, dribbling the ball with my feet using some of the footwork I had learned in dance.

Then, out of the corner of my eye, I saw an opposing player running toward me. I clocked

Tanner, but he was completely surrounded. I looked around, but there was no one else near me. I shifted my weight as another player came at me and tried to steal the ball. I easily outmaneuvered him and continued my streak up the field. The player coming at me from the side had almost reached me, and the goal was straight ahead. I saw the player drop down and slide, clearly intending to trip me, take me down and steal the ball.

I didn't even slow down. My heartbeat was steady, sounding like a drumbeat in my ears. I got my foot under the ball and launched it upward, then followed it. I leaped up, using my arms and tightening my muscles to propel me forward. I flew over my opponent. I jumped so high that I glanced down and saw the other boy staring up at me in total shock. I landed solidly, right behind the ball, and took two steps forward before firing the side of my foot forward and sending the ball flying past the goalie and directly into the back of the net. It was the winning goal!

The crowd went absolutely wild. They were on their feet in the stands, screaming. My teammates ran down the field and grabbed me.

"That was unbelievable!" Aiden screamed.

"Dude, that jump was unreal!" Tanner yelled, slapping me on the back.

I looked at the stands and saw my parents standing with Jen, clapping wildly as Jen waved a hand-lettered sign that said, *Go, John, Go!* I grinned and waved at them as the team celebrated our victory.

"Nice job, McCaffrey!" the coach yelled over the din. "Looks like all that dancing paid off!"

"Thanks, Coach," I called before my teammates hoisted me onto their shoulders and carried me around the field.

It was just like in a movie.

Twenty-Five

I was managing to juggle soccer, practice for the Cultural Center and keep up with my homework. At this point, everyone in school knew about my dancing. Tanner really had done me a favor. I didn't have to hide anymore, and the range of reactions from people was kind of funny. Kids I didn't even know came up and told me they thought it was kind of cool. Jen decided she might like to take the class with Santee and the girls sometime. The librarian pressed a couple of books into my hands about the history of First Nations people and their celebrations. There was still the odd idiot...like the racist jerk who started whooping and dancing around me in the hallway. But I just kept walking, and Aiden checked the kid into the wall with his shoulder. It was kind of worth it to see the look on the kid's face when he bounced off the wall. Aside from rare instances like that, people were actually pretty cool.

Like my math teacher, Mr. Beckham. He had handed back my algebra quiz along with a high five that morning.

"Good job, John. Nice to see you can solve equations as well as you multitask. Really good work."

I liked Mr. Beckham and grinned back at him. "Thanks, sir. I try."

The fact was, I was doing pretty well, all things considered. But the next day was Saturday—time to go back to the Cultural Center for the Pow Wow group. I was beyond nervous. I had started to second-guess the backflip, and I was still stumbling on some of the tricks. I kept running through my routine in my head and messing up the sequence of the steps.

It was late. Or early, depending how you looked at it. The moon was huge and full, and it lit up the backyard with a soft glow that made the lawn look like it was alive. I stepped into the backyard and stopped, feeling the grass under my bare feet. I put earbuds into my ears and strapped my iPod to my arm. I closed my eyes and ran my fingers down the cord, pressing *Play* and waiting for the familiar drumbeats to start pounding their way into my head and flowing down through my body.

Under the full moon, I heard the music. I felt it. And with no one watching and no concern about the boys at the Cultural Center, I opened my eyes and started to dance.

Twenty-Six

I had spent the early hours of Saturday morning drinking coffee and pushing scrambled eggs around a plate, picking at a piece of toast and nibbling a fruit salad in turn. I ate almost none of it.

"Did you sleep?" my mother asked, walking into the kitchen and cinching her robe tightly around her waist.

"Not much," I admitted, holding out my coffee mug for a refill. She glanced at it, then at my face, as if trying to gauge my caffeine level. She must have deemed it acceptable because she stood over me and filled up the mug.

"Hey." My father walked in and pulled his favorite chipped blue mug out of the cupboard over the sink. "Did you get any sleep?"

I exchanged glances with my mother, who winked at me and shrugged.

"Not much. I couldn't sleep, so I was up early running through my routine." I put my cup down on the table and took a deep breath, willing my hands to stop shaking. I wasn't sure anymore if it was nerves or caffeine causing that.

My father sat down across from me and leaned over, putting his hands on my knees. He was usually a man of few words, but he looked me in the eye proudly and nodded.

"You've got this, son. Remember who you are." He patted my leg again and stood up, taking his coffee cup with him as he left the room. I raised an eyebrow at my mom as Jen walked into the room. I was surprised my father had even that much to say before his morning coffee. His words resonated, but before I had a chance to think much about them, Jen's voice cut into my reverie.

"So? Ready to go in front of a bunch of racist jackoffs and dance your butt off?" she asked, biting into a chocolate-chip muffin.

"Jen!" my mother and I both yelled.

I stifled a laugh. "They're not all so bad," I told her. "But yeah...I don't know. I'm second-guessing the flip." All I could imagine was trying to flip, falling short and landing on my head.

"Shake it off, bro. You'll be fine." She was being flippant, but she didn't know how big a deal this was. It could make or break my experience at the Cultural Center and determine whether I stayed or not. And it scared the hell out of me. She glanced away from picking the chocolate chips out of her muffin and adding them to the pile on the edge of her plate and saw my terrified expression. "John! I didn't mean to freak you out! Do you need a paper bag to breathe into or something?"

"No." I held a hand up in front of me. "I'll be okay." I tried to take a deep breath, but I couldn't seem to get enough air into my lungs.

"Mom!" Jen yelled, jumping up from the table and dropping her muffin. "John's dying or something!" She ran around the table to me. "Put your head between your knees, John! Here! Breathe into this!" Jen grabbed the bag her muffin had been in and thrust it into my hands.

Mom ran over to me. "Jen! Stop manhandling him."

I breathed deeply into the paper bag, the smell of chocolate-chip muffins filling my nose.

That actually made it worse. Now I felt like I was going to throw up too. I sat up and pushed the bag into Jen's hands while my mother rubbed my back.

"I'm okay. I'm okay," I told her. "I just...realized how much I have to lose. And how much I want to stay there and learn." I tried again to keep my hands from shaking.

"Are you sure you want to do this?" my mother asked, looking at me worriedly.

"Yeah. I'm good." I tried to sound convincing.

It must have worked, because my mother nodded. "Okay then. Good." She looked at the clock and then flew to her feet. "Oh my goodness! Gct dressed! We should have left by now! Jennifer!" She spun toward Jen, who had a forkful of fruit halfway to her mouth.

She dropped it in surprise. "What?" She hopped off her stool and grabbed a paper towel to clean up the fruit.

"Get ready! We have to leave in five minutes!"

Jen rolled her eyes and sauntered out of the room.

"John!"

"Right here, Mom."

"Get dressed! We're going to be late!"

"I *am* dressed. I've been dressed for hours," I told her, sipping at my bitter coffee.

"Oh. Good. Okay then."

"Mom?" I said.

"Yes?"

"*You* should get dressed."

"Oh!" She looked down at her robe. "Yes! I will." She kissed my cheek. "I'm proud of you, John."

"Thanks, Mom," I said as she ran off to get dressed.

Twenty-Seven

My stomach was in knots the entire ride into the city. I even decided to forgo my usual hot chocolate and maple-dip donut at the obligatory stop at Tim Hortons. My father was driving and my mom was singing along to the radio while my sister talked about her latest art project and how she thought she might like to try a dance class sometime. I was too anxious to talk much.

"Are you nervous, nikosis?" my mother asked, craning around in her seat to look at me. I shrugged at her, not trusting myself to speak. I felt like I was going to throw up. But I had worked day and night to perfect a routine—and my family was going to be there for moral support. And we were going to show Matt once and for all that I belonged there just as much as he did.

My father pulled into the parking lot of the Cultural Center, and I took a deep breath, trying to calm my nerves. I was ready for this.

I couldn't wait to see the look on Matt's face.

I walked into the studio and stood beside Jasper. "Hey." I nodded at him. "Pow Wow's coming up."

He lifted his eyebrows in response.

"Think you'll go?" I asked.

"Yeah," he replied. "Not to compete," he quickly added. "Maybe in another year. But I always go for the Grand Entry." He looked around the room, maybe to see if Matt was lurking around to catch him talking to me. Or maybe just to see if we were about to start. "Are you going?"

"Yeah. I've never danced in a Pow Wow before. I've been to a bunch of them. But I've always just watched."

Jasper nodded. "You'll really like it," he said. The room was filling up with boys, and for some reason, Jasper was still talking to me. Matt was standing off to the side with a few of his friends, stretching, when my father walked in.

"Dad!" I called out. "Hey, Dad, over here!" I waved my arm in the air as if we were in a crowd of hundreds instead of a room with a dozen boys in it. Jasper looked at me with a slight frown, probably thinking I was crazy. Matt poked one of his friends and started laughing. Exactly what I had expected.

"Dad, this is Jasper."

My father smiled at him.

"Nice to meet you, sir." Jasper politely shook his hand.

"Looks like we're being taken over by white people!" I heard Matt tell his friends. "Next thing you know, they'll be sending us off to school, trying to colonize us!" A couple of his friends laughed, but some of them looked away uncomfortably. My grandfather had been in a residential school. I suspected the other boys had relatives who'd been in the schools too. It wasn't funny.

"Mr. McCaffrey!" Sam called out, walking over and holding out his hand. "Glad you could join us. Everyone, this is John's father."

"No kidding," Matt muttered.

"John, is the rest of your family joining us?"

Before I could say anything, Matt interrupted. "Isn't this the *Native* Cultural Center?" he asked. "I mean, we've put up with this guy playing Indian for weeks, but now we have to entertain his family too? How pale is this place going to get?"

"Matt!" Sam started, but I cut him off, striding away from my father to stand directly in front of Matt.

"I've had enough of your racist comments," I told him.

He looked at me, startled.

"You've been insulting me since the day I got here, and you don't know anything about me. I have as much right to be here as you do. My mother..." I looked around for her and Jen, and saw them standing by the door. I gestured toward them. "My mother's maiden name is Greyeyes. She's Cree. *Nihtâ-nîmihitow.* That means 'She dances well.'"

Matt looked absolutely shocked.

"*Miyokosisâniwiw,*" my mother said. I knew what that meant: *He is a fine son.*

I nodded at her proudly. "These are my dances too," I told Matt. "I let you take that away from me, but not anymore."

Twenty-Eight

They had started the same way they always did, shuffling around in a circle and moving to the drums. My mother, sister and even my father joined us in the circle, tapping their feet and stepping forward with the group. When we stopped moving, I was the first one to step into the middle. I stood still for a minute and closed my eyes, listening.

I waited for my cue, opened my eyes and took three running steps before leaping into the air. I fell back to earth and began to spin, lifting my knees and stomping my feet. I shifted my weight suddenly and dropped down onto my right hand, kicking both of my feet up into the air before pivoting my hips back down. I barely registered the group cheering as I kept dancing. My knees were high as I spun around and then sank down into the splits before using the muscles in my legs and abs to push myself back up to standing. The roar of the group followed me as I kept dancing, kept spinning and turning on one foot, then the other. I was almost at the end. I had almost reached the climax of the number. The drums and voices got louder, and I slid to a stop right in front of Matt before gathering myself, tensing my muscles and leaping into a perfectly executed backflip, just like Jen had taught me. I landed it with razor-sharp precision as the drumbeats ended.

I heard the gasps, followed by cheering, as my family, Sam and the other boys erupted in applause. I stood still, breathing hard and taking the moment in. I had done it. I had shown everyone that I belonged there. I had held my head up high and danced my heart out.

I had remembered who I was.

MELANIE FLORENCE is of Cree and Scottish descent. She is the author of the OLA Best Bets award-winning book *Righting Canada's Wrongs: Residential Schools; Missing Nimama*, which was awarded an Honourable Mention by the OLA; *The Missing, One Night*; and *Jordin Tootoo: The Highs and Lows in the Journey of the First Inuk to Play in the NHL*, which was chosen as an Honor Book by The American Indian Library Association. Melanie works as a freelance journalist and her byline has appeared in numerous magazines, including *Dance International, Writer Magazine, Parents Canada* and *Urban Male Magazine*. She currently lives in Toronto with her family.

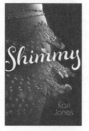